THE DEVLIN AFFAIR

4. 7

DOUBLE FASTBACK®
M Y S T E R Y

THE DEVLIN AFFAIR

DAN J. MARLOWE

Globe Fearon Education Publisher
Upper Saddle River, New Jersey
www.globefearon.com

DOUBLE FASTBACK® MYSTERY Books

The Actress
Brannigan's Folly
Death at the Border
The Devlin Affair
Family Reunion
The Lost Train
The Night Marchers
The Sleepers
Vanished
Voices in the Night

Cover photographer: Richard Hutchings

ISBN 0-8224-2362-6

Library of Congress Catalog Card Number: 86-81003

Printed in the United States of America.

1. 10 9 8 7 6

My close friends—all three of them—call me Dev. The full name is Lew Devlin. I'm a private eye in San Diego. I work for an outfit called the Timmerman Protective Agency, and I've been with them for four years.

My boss is Joe Timmerman. He's called "the Old Warrior" around the agency, but not where he can hear it. He has bronze skin, a bristling white crew cut, and a face with lines in it that are deep enough to hold three days' rain.

Our agency specializes in industrial spying. We protect our client companies against other companies who are trying to steal their formulas or processes or other business secrets.

That's our main area, but every once in a while we end up in a different corner of the ring. That's why I was sitting on the other side of Joe Timmerman's desk this particular morning. He'd just told me I was taking a noon flight today to Washington, D.C. I was to pick up a suitcase at the FBI Building and deliver it to an address in Mexico City.

"The FBI Building," I repeated.

"That's right," Timmerman said. "They asked for you."

I used to be an FBI agent. I left because if you're not out in the field, it's just like any other nine-to-five job. I don't like to know exactly what I'll be doing at 10:30 each morning. Or at 3:30 each afternoon. The FBI had me planning operations. When I asked to be included in the operations, the brass stood me off. So I quit.

"The FBI can't work in Mexico City or anywhere else out of the country," I said. Timmerman nodded. He knew it as well as I did. I was really just thinking out loud. "But they're obviously into something down there and want to be covered on a transfer of some kind. Why us?"

"I don't know. But they asked for you," Timmerman said again. "And the fee is right."

I knew that was the important reason as far as he was concerned. "Who talked to you?"

"A guy named Cartwright. He sounded like a big wheel. Or at least he thinks he is."

I knew Jim Cartwright. He'd send flowers to your funeral *if* they were paid for by his agency. He was a hard guy, Mr. Cartwright—strictly a 20-minute egg. It wasn't comforting to be working for a guy like that in a job that might not be quite legal.

"I'm not very fond of Mexican jails," I told Timmerman.

"They'd get you out," he assured me.

"When—in six or eight years? Anyway, I'm down on the office calendar for a week's trout fishing in Colorado."

"The trout will still be there when you get back." Timmerman leaned back in his chair and folded his hands behind his head. "They asked for you, Devlin," he said for the third time. His dark eyes bored into mine. "How much good is it going to do the Timmerman Agency if I insist you're not available?"

Three hours later I was on the noon flight to Washington.

It was 7:30 P.M. Washington time when my plane landed at National Airport. I took a cab to the Hay-Adams Hotel and checked in. I had a steak at Duke Zeibert's and a chocolate sundae at the Mayflower Hotel Coffee Shop. They had always had the best sundaes in town.

The next morning I walked down Pennsylvania Avenue to the FBI Building. I waited 40 minutes outside Jim Cartwright's office before he was ready to see me. That's the name of the game in Washington.

When I was finally admitted to the inner office, I decided that Cartwright hadn't changed, at least in appearance. He still looked like a 20-minute egg.

He gave me a nod but no verbal greeting. Very few ex-agents receive a warm welcome back at the Bureau. After all, if an ex-agent were a hundred cents on the dollar, he'd still be with the FBI, right?

Cartwright picked up a tan suitcase and set it down on top of his desk. He opened it with a key and showed me that it was empty. "Fill that up with bulky clothing and deliver it to the Excelsior Hotel in Mexico City, Devlin."

I knew the suitcase had a false bottom and whatever I was delivering was in that false bottom. And I knew that Cartwright knew I knew. "Is there a story that goes along with the package?" I asked.

"Not for you, Devlin. Just deliver it."

It was the typical attitude that always bothered me in Washington. "Do I deliver it to the hotel barbershop?"

His eyes narrowed. Jim Cartwright didn't like wise guys. I had heard him say so often enough. "The desk clerk at the Excelsior will have a room for you," he told me. "And a man will come to your room this evening and pick up the bag."

"Six feet two, eyes of blue?"

The narrowed eyes came down another notch. "Five feet six, and he'll be Mexican. He'll tell you he's come for the paper."

"The paper," I repeated.

Cartwright handed me the suitcase key after locking it again. He started shuffling papers on his desk. Apparently our conversation had ended. When I picked up the suitcase, it felt pretty heavy. I'd need some really bulky clothing to make the fully loaded suitcase look okay to Mexican customs. And that would make the entire thing very heavy.

The last thing Cartwright handed me was an airline ticket. I put it in my coat pocket, picked up the suitcase, and walked toward the door. Behind me I heard Cartwright clear his throat. But if he'd been about to say something he changed his mind.

I took a cab back to the hotel. I put the tan FBI suitcase on my bed, unlocked it, and popped the hidden latches. I lifted out the panel that concealed the false bottom. Inside were bundles of foreign currency. A lot of foreign currency, plus some stiff-feeling papers. I picked up a half dozen and examined them. They were stock certificates and bonds.

I hadn't expected Cabbage Patch dolls, but it still made me think. The Mexican government is especially touchy about money coming in or going out of their country. They like to control the flow. All the cash on the bed right before my eyes made me a little angry, too. It annoyed me that Cartwright hadn't seen fit to let me know what the actual program was going to be.

I replaced the money and other valuables inside the false bottom of the suitcase. I hadn't brought enough clothes with me to make the suitcase look as full as it should be to account for its weight. I went downstairs to the men's shop in the hotel lobby and bought two topcoats. I crammed them into the suitcase on top of my own things. When I picked it up, the weight didn't seem out of line with what I had piled into it.

I took a cab to the airport. I had three scrambled eggs and an order of hash browns while I waited for my plane.

Four hours later I was feeling disgusted. The Aeromexico 707 to which I transferred in Dallas had come up with a mechanical problem. The pilot had been forced to land at an out-of-the-way airstrip halfway to Mexico City. After an hour on the ground, I overheard two passengers say that the flight engineer had found the problem and finally fixed it.

But that wasn't a cure for our situation. The landing strip was a privately built runway designed for use by the small aircraft of a mining company. One look was enough to show that nothing larger than a Gulfstream or a DC-3 could take off on the short runway. Our fully passenger-loaded 707 had no chance. We had to wait for Aeromexico to route in two smaller planes before we could complete our trip.

All of the passengers were waiting in a tin-roofed coffee shop about 100 yards from the runway. The scruffy-looking room was filled with strange odors, not all of them pleasant. A dozen small tables were scattered about the room. Chatter in a half dozen languages could be heard, much of it in Spanish. Spanish is not one of my strong points.

I joined the coffee line that had formed near the counter. I placed the suitcase at my feet and nudged it along with my knee as the line moved forward. *"Cafe con leche, por favor,"* I said to the stout woman behind the counter. The phrase used up about a third of my Spanish vocabulary.

The woman handed me my coffee with milk in a thick white mug with a spoon already standing in it. I looked for one of the tiny two-place tables I'd noticed in the corner. Only one of them had an empty seat. A slender woman was sitting alone, reading a thick, black-covered book. It appeared to be a Bible or a prayer book.

She looked up from her reading and saw me standing there. She spoke up at once, pointing to the empty chair at her table. "Please sit down if you like," she said in a pleasant voice.

"Ahhhh, you speak English!" I said in relief.

Her smooth skin had a golden tan. Her black hair was shoulder length. She wore a dark skirt and a cotton blouse. I couldn't see any makeup or jewelry. At her feet was a large canvas carrying case covered with zipper-fastened compartments and pockets. It was fitted with a carrying handle and shoulder straps.

By the time I sat down, the woman had returned her attention to her book. I had first guessed that she was in her early twenties. At close range I could see I'd have to add ten years to that. She had a calm expression that indicated she wasn't a first-time traveler. I made out the word *Poesía* on the spine of her book. Poetry? Yes, that was probably it. She looked like the kind of person who would read poetry.

An hour passed. I was almost ready to risk my fourth cup of coffee when I saw two twin-engined planes land, one behind the other. The copilot of our downed 707 came into the coffee shop. He announced in English and Spanish that we would be boarding the new planes soon. He directed the passengers to gather outside at the edge of the runway with their luggage.

I picked up my suitcase and went out to join the others. Directly behind me was my table companion. She carried her heavy-looking case easily. Two flight attendants stood at the head of the line of passengers, checking them aboard the planes.

I heard a bang-bang close by. I realized that the sounds were gunshots. When I turned in the direction of the sounds, I could see a large, dark dog loping along the edge of the airstrip. The dog was being pursued by a battered, dust-covered jeep. The driver was spinning the wheel furiously, trying to avoid potholes, but the jeep was bouncing in and out of them.

A uniformed man stood beside the driver with his elbows propped on top of the windshield. He was holding a gun in his hands. The two men were wearing sweat-stained khaki pants with gun belts. Sunlight flashed from badges pinned to their shirt pockets.

The man with the weapon fired at the dog. The bullet missed and flew over the heads of the waiting passengers. A tremor ran through the line. "Down!" I said sharply, hoping everyone could hear me. I dropped full-length upon the ground.

"Cuidado! Cuidado! Perro rabioso!" the jeep's driver was shouting excitedly.

"Mad dog," the woman from the coffee shop said quietly behind me.

Most of the passengers dropped to the ground. The man with the weapon held his fire, apparently aware for the first time of the nearness of the passengers. I climbed to my feet and got out of my jacket quickly. I started to wrap it around my left arm.

The movement caught the dog's eye and it charged at me. I could see all too plainly its bared teeth and the yellowish foam dripping from its jaws. The animal's deep-throated growls were almost as loud as the noisy transmission of the pursuing jeep.

The jeep was gaining, but not quickly enough. I crouched with my left arm extended and braced myself. Then a canvas case came sailing over my shoulder. It landed in the path of the rabid dog. The animal swerved and slowed down, but it picked up speed again almost at once. It took me a second to realize that the woman passenger from the coffee shop had thrown her case at the dog.

The dog was nearly in my face when I felt my suitcase jerked away from where I had a leg braced against it. I whirled, but the bag was already in the air, heading straight at the dog. The suitcase struck it in the side and knocked it over. The animal twisted, snapping at the case. Then the suit-case and dog both ended up beneath the wheels of the brake-locked, skidding, dust-raising jeep.

The man with the gun leaped down from his position beside the driver. The dog was badly hurt but it was still alive. It was trying to crawl out from underneath the jeep. Keeping his distance, the uniformed man aimed carefully and sent a bullet through the dog's diseased brain. Fortunately he shot away from the direction of the crowd, which by that time had scattered in several directions.

The jeep's driver jumped down and shook hands with his companion. A murmur rose from the passengers around me. I knew what had caused the stir because I was looking right at it. One end of the FBI suitcase, still under the jeep, had been crushed. A seam had split in the false bottom and some 20 loose bills were fluttering along the ground. More bank notes were sticking out of the suitcase's broken bottom panel. Ten-thousand-peso Mexican bills blew around on the sandy soil with British pounds, Swiss francs, West German marks, and Japanese yen.

Both the sound of the crowd and the direction in which the people were staring attracted the attention of the uniformed men. The gunman knelt down and looked under the jeep. He shouted something to his companion. Then he crawled farther underneath and began to pull my suitcase out into the open.

I had to stop that. I dropped down behind him and grabbed him by the ankles. His head made a "thunking" sound when it struck the undercarriage as I dragged him out. "Look out!" the woman from the coffee shop called to me.

I knew where to look. The second khaki-clad man was running around the front of the jeep to get to me. His holster was buttoned down, but he was clawing at it to get his automatic in his hand. He had to pass the woman before he could reach me. As he went by, she put out a foot and tripped him. It really surprised me. The guy

sprawled out facedown almost at my feet.
I neck-chopped him twice, and he lay there,
out cold like his friend.

I scrambled to each of them in turn,
removing their hardware. I didn't really
want the pistols, but I couldn't let them
have them, either. My back felt itchy by the
time I straightened up again. I had the guns,
but I didn't have control. There were too
many people, and nothing said they had to
be on my side. Human nature said that in
another moment or two someone would do
something foolish. Was I supposed to blast
an otherwise innocent person attracted by
the sight of the FBI's money?

I didn't even know where I was. I had
some recollection of a crew member saying
we were about halfway between the border
and Mexico City. Considering the route we

took from Dallas, that meant we were probably somewhere between Saltillo and San Luis Potosí. Right now, though, we were in the middle of nowhere. How do you plan for someone throwing your suit-case under the wheels of a jeep?

My brain seemed frozen in neutral. The crowd pulled back another pace or two at the sight of the weapons I had collected. I heard the woman's voice again. "Into the jeep!" she yelled. She was on the far side of the jeep, bending over and pulling my suit-case from beneath it. She stuffed what she could of the loose-dangling bills back inside. Then she swung the suitcase into the back of the jeep.

Right behind it came her own bag. The jeep's engine was still idling. I scrambled into the driver's seat. Both of us ignored

the loose money on the edge of the runway. I threw the jeep into gear and sped
away.

Within the first ten yards we went into
and out of a huge pothole. We bounced so
high I thought I'd broken my neck. Then I
saw two more jeeps proceeding along the
far edge of the runway.

"They're speeding up," my copilot
announced. She didn't sound too excited
about it. She was stating a fact. I spun the
jeep's steering wheel and began a broken-
field run through the mining company's
other buildings beyond the coffee shop.

"They've stopped beside the men back
there," the woman said.

"I hope picking up the loose cash slows
them down," I said. I glanced across the
jeep's front seat at her. "I apologize for not
planning my getaway better than this."

"The apology should come from me," she said. "I panicked when I saw the dog coming at us." I couldn't believe it; she was smiling. "Where do you find a bank with so many kinds of foreign money?" she continued.

"I'd prefer not saying." I had run out of mining company buildings to dodge behind. I set sail across open country at the best clip I could manage without rolling the jeep over. "Am I heading north?"

She squinted at the sun. "I'd say so."

North led to the U.S. border. Since I'd just committed a number of crimes against the Mexican code of justice, that seemed the right direction to be heading. With no publicity, of course. That would be required by Jim Cartwright.

Thinking of the FBI official reminded me that I was supposed to be heading south, not north. I could almost hear Joe Timmerman's harsh voice in my ear telling me that same thing.

I looked across at the woman again. I didn't even know her name. "I'm Lew Devlin," I said.

"I'm Angela Baker." She was looking back over her shoulder. "Here they come again."

I risked a quick glance backward. Two rising dust clouds were evidence of pursuit. I knew I couldn't outdrive Mexican nationals in their own kind of country. I had to do something more positive than trying to run away from them. Angela confirmed that thought in almost the same instant. "They're gaining," she said.

I took another glance backward. The pursuing jeeps were much closer. More than that, they had spread out so I couldn't attempt an end run. It was time to make a move. Maybe past time.

"Move over here beside me," I told Angela. She did so at once. "Put your left foot down on the gas." I felt her foot searching for the pedal before it settled down. "Okay. Hands on the steering wheel. Try not to flip us."

I twisted toward the rear, holding one of the pistols. I did a double take when I saw how close the pursuit was. Even above the sound of the hard-racing engines I could hear the pop-pop of gunfire. Then a bullet clanged off our jeep.

I leveled my captured pistol at the nearest jeep and snapped off two shots at its radiator. A spurt of dust and then of water indicated that one had connected. I turned my attention to the second jeep. If it had slowed down and followed at a distance, we might not have made it. But the second jeep's driver wanted to be a hero. When he saw his partner fall back with a bullet in his radiator, the second driver came charging directly at us.

I fired at the second radiator but with no result that I could see. A khaki-clad uniform was standing up and shooting at us. I heard a bullet smash into the undercarriage of our jeep. I fired once more at our remaining opponent. An instant after I did, something came crashing into my right shoulder. It turned me around so violently that I was almost facing the dashboard again.

I knew it was a bullet, and I knew it had hit bone. Pain flashed through my entire body right down to my toes. My eyes flooded with tears. Angela, concentrating on her steering, hadn't noticed.

I tried to pull myself together. I blinked my eyes clear and turned to look backward again. The twisting movement sent another jolt of pain through my shoulder. My look back gave me some comfort, though. The second jeep had also broken off pursuit and was veering away from us in a long arc. There was a welcome sight of escaping steam coming from its radiator, too.

I faced forward again. I placed the automatic on the seat and then reached for the steering wheel with my left hand. "Okay, I'll drive," I said to Angela. It didn't come out sounding nearly as strong as I'd wanted.

She released the wheel and looked at me. "Oh!" she exclaimed when she saw my right shoulder. Drops of blood were trickling down my arm and puddling in the crease of my elbow. "Pull over," she said. "I'll bandage that."

"Got to get out of sight first," I grunted. My vision was blurring. I was steering us into as many potholes as I was avoiding. I took a quick look at the sky. There were probably another two hours of daylight left.

Angela stood up in the bounding jeep and reached into the back. She lifted her canvas case from the rear and sat down with it in her lap. It was the second indication I'd had that she was no 97-pound weakling. The way she'd thrown her case and mine at the rabid dog had been an eye-opener, too.

She unzipped a side pocket on her case and pulled out a green metal box with a large Red Cross showing on it.

"You're a doctor?" I said hoarsely.

"I'm a nurse."

She didn't add any details. I had intended to drive for an hour, but I didn't last that long. In less than half that time I was grinding my teeth every time the jeep's wheels touched down. Up ahead I could see we were approaching a dip that led between two small hills. I steered into it thankfully. At least it would keep us from being as visible as a fly in a bowl of milk.

I stopped in the shade of a yucca tree with a twisted trunk. Angela jumped down from the jeep and circled it swiftly. I eased myself down slowly. "There's a 20-gallon water tank attached to the rear," she said. "Intact."

That was good news. It was great news. Without water in this dry countryside we would have been in a bad way. "Sit down," she said, motioning toward the shade. "Take your shirt off."

I managed it, gritting my teeth again. Cool fingertips examined my wound. "The bullet grazed the bone and took out a small chunk of skin," Angela stated.

"Grazed? You mean it *hit* the bone. I'm the world's greatest living expert on that subject."

She smiled and set to work. Within 15 minutes the shoulder was bandaged and my right arm was in a makeshift sling. I was also wearing the bloodstained shirt again, draped loosely over my shoulders.

When I looked Angela's way again, she was scanning the sky. "Helicopters," she said. "They could come after us. It depends on how mad the police are."

"They don't have to be mad," I pointed out. "They just have to be after the money they saw."

"The ones after us were *federales*. National police. I could tell by their uniforms."

"Lovely," I said. "When can we expect to see the tanks?"

She smiled again, half-mocking, half-serious. She had a very nice smile. "You have a very nice smile," I told her. "You should show it more often. Otherwise you look too serious."

She didn't say anything. She climbed up into the jeep, rummaged around in the back, and jumped down with a machete in her hand. She walked along the nearby hillside, swinging the machete at bunches of coarse grass. Then she gathered it up and spread it over the jeep in a form of camouflage.

"I should have thought of that," I said.

Angela went back to her case and unzipped another compartment. From it she removed a small radio not much larger than a cigarette package. She switched it on, and then faced in different directions while she listened.

"Nothing," she said, clicking it off. "I'll try it again after dark. Radio stations have greater range after sundown."

"You think we made the headlines?"

She wasn't smiling when she replied. "How could we not?"

It made me realize the position she was trapped in while in my company. "We'll find a village tomorrow," I said. "Then I'll drop you off close by so you can walk to it.

You speak the language. You can blend in."
I stopped because she was shaking her head.

"It's too late for that," she responded.

"Why?"

"We were seen sitting together and talking in the coffee shop. We were standing together in the boarding line when the new planes came. Everyone saw that you didn't have to slug me to get me into the jeep. The second *federale* knows who tripped him. The Mexican police—well, you know what they'll think."

"That we're together," I said slowly. "But there's got to be a way—" I stopped because I couldn't think of a way.

"It's not important," she said.

"It's important not to get caught until we get this mess straightened out." I tried to sit up straighter and winced.

Angela made no reply. She went back to her bottomless canvas case again and removed a shallow pot and two aluminum mugs. Within five minutes she had an almost smokeless fire blazing from twigs of mesquite. She dumped four small cans she had opened into the pot.

I took the mug of thick, hot soup she handed me and gulped it down. "You continue to amaze me, lady," I said sincerely. "What are you doing in Mexico?"

"I'm applying for a job in Mexico City."

"I see. You know, that's one thing wrong with the status of this current trip. We're both going to Mexico City, but we're actually heading away from it. We're going to have to have a council of war about that."

"When you're feeling better."

"I don't feel too bad," I lied.

She shook her head knowingly. "A wound like yours is a shock to the whole system. Five hundred yards in the jeep would break the wound wide open again. We'll stay here tonight and tomorrow and start again tomorrow night."

I began to argue and then stopped. Who was I trying to kid? I knew a few ten-year-olds who were probably stronger than I felt right then. Twenty-four hours of rest might leave me feeling almost human again.

Angela switched on her radio again and pivoted as she aimed it in different directions. I heard a couple of weak Spanish-speaking voices against the background of music. Then she found a stronger voice that spoke at some length. By listening closely, I heard our names mentioned a few times.

Angela's expression didn't change. "Bad?" I asked when she silenced the radio.

"Not good," she admitted.

"What's the problem?" I asked. As if I didn't know.

"The police are searching the state of San Luis Potosí for the American criminals. But they think we're a hundred miles farther north."

"That's good. Especially when we head south. One thing, though. We've got to get rid of the jeep."

She raised an eyebrow. "You don't think that most Mexicans will stay away from an official-looking jeep?"

"It's a point. But we'll also be more noticeable riding around in it. We shouldn't risk it if we have a choice."

The conversation ended. The night chill from the high desert was already making me feel worse. I tossed Angela my keys. "There are two topcoats in my suitcase," I told her. "We'll need them before morning."

Even with the topcoats it was a rugged night. I woke up several times and had a hard time getting back to sleep. In the morning I felt about as well as if someone had rolled a tractor over me all night. Angela supplied coffee from her canvas case and made a new fire. Neither of us said anything, but we were both rationing water from the tank on the jeep.

During the long hot day that followed we each did a few things necessary to get ready for our trip that night. Angela patched up my suitcase with wide strips of tape from her medical kit. I checked out the jeep's engine.

Just before dark she rebandaged my shoulder. Then we reloaded the jeep and started out. I headed east. It was a clear night with a three-quarter moon. I could see fairly well. Driving conditions were just as bad as before, though. And once I drove into a dead-end gully and we had to back-track for three miles.

After driving for several hours, I voiced a thought that had been with me for a while. "This creeping along cross-country isn't going to get the job done, Angela. It could take us a week this way." What I couldn't tell her was that I couldn't be a week late for my meeting in Mexico City. "We've got to find a road heading south. Even if it's a dirt road, it should eventually lead us to a highway."

I thought she might object, but she said nothing. I drove on over the teeth-rattling ground. An hour later we came to a break in our hilly desert surroundings: a dirt road running roughly north-south. I stopped the jeep, switched off the lights, and once again considered our limited options.

Nothing had changed that I could see. There was no visible traffic on the dirt road. Mexican automobile traffic drops quite a bit at night. Horses, cows, and other animals wandering around loose tend to discourage traffic after dark.

I shrugged and looked across the front seat at Angela. In the moonlight I could see that she was smiling. "Go for it," she said.

"You've got it," I told her.

I turned the headlights back on and headed south on the dirt road. Within the first 20 yards the headlights picked up a white hand-painted sign at the edge of the road. I couldn't read it. By the time I had the jeep stopped again, Angela was handing me a flashlight from her carrying case.

I jumped down from the jeep and walked over to the sign. The sign said Matehuala, 15 kilometers. I went back to the jeep and handed Angela her flashlight.

"Matehuala is about nine miles from here," I explained to her. "I've been there before. It's on Highway 57, one of the main routes south from the border. It's north of the city of San Luis Potosí, the state capital. From Matehuala I guess it's another 350 miles to Mexico City."

"That's not too bad," Angela said.

So we started out again. The dirt road was quite rough. During the rainy season it must resemble a muddy creek bed. But it was dry now, and the jeep managed it well.

Before too long I saw a glow ahead of us in the sky. "Matehuala," I said. "It's no great city, but out here in the dark countryside any kind of civilization looks like Times Square."

Ten minutes later we began passing scattered small houses. A couple of dirt side roads fed into ours. Then abruptly I saw a moving dark blur on the right. I went for the brake. But a loud metallic scraping sound announced that we had been hit by another vehicle. Wherever it had come from, I was positive it hadn't had any lights on.

The jeep skidded to a stop. I jumped down and began to walk back up the road. I could see a fender-wrinkled passenger car partway across the road. It looked like a ten-year-old Pontiac.

A man was walking toward me. "So sorry, señor," he was saying. "It is my error."

"Where were your lights?" I demanded hotly as we came face-to-face.

"Señor, I must explain to you—"

I never even saw his arm move. Just *Pow!* and a bright white light exploded behind my eyes. I hadn't taken a sucker punch to the jaw like that since my army days. I found myself on my back in the dusty roadway.

My opponent leaned over me, which was a mistake on his part. I kicked at his face, but he dodged. Then I kicked at his knee and connected. He squawked and sat down in the road. We both got to our feet at the same time.

I missed a couple of punches but then landed a few. I could see his face start to break up. He began to retreat. Then another voice raised itself behind me. "Hola, Jaime! Look at *this!*"

I hit my man again and he went down into a ditch. I whirled to see what was going on behind me. Angela was out of the jeep. The other man was advancing on her, a huge grin showing white teeth beneath a bushy mustache. I started to run toward them.

I needn't have bothered. Angela picked up the front of her skirt in both hands, did a fast spin on one leg, and slammed the shoe of her other foot against the guy's ear. He went sideways six feet in my direction. I grabbed him and hit him once to make sure, although I don't think he really needed it. When I let go of him, he went right down into the dirt.

"*Bandidos,*" Angela said.

"Bandits?" I asked.

"Yes. They create incidents to get cars to stop and then they rob the drivers and passengers. Not on the main highways, which are police patrolled, but in areas like this."

"Let's get these amateurs tied up," I said. "I want to see if their car is any good."

"They'll have rope in their car," she said.

They did. We tied them up quickly. Then I hurried back to their car. The key was in the ignition. I started the engine and listened closely. It didn't sound too bad.

Angela leaned in the window beside me. "You want to change vehicles here, Devlin?"

"When will we ever have a better chance?"

We didn't debate the issue. We transferred our things to the car, whose fuel gauge showed the tank was half-full. I loaded the bandits into the jeep and drove the jeep off the road and behind a hill. Someone would find them eventually, but not too soon, I hoped.

Dawn was cracking the eastern sky when I headed the car down the road toward Matehuala.

Once we hit Highway 57 we made much better time. Around 7:30 we stopped in Matehuala for breakfast.

After we ate, we both realized how tired we were. Rather than risk stopping at any hotel, we pulled off the main streets and parked near a deserted warehouse. Then we just slept in the car for a few hours.

Around 11:00 we hit the road again. It took us a little more than an hour to reach San Luis Potosí. I was glad to get beyond it, because just south of it we passed into the smaller state of Guanajuato. Mexican authorities don't like to let local problems carry to other jurisdictions. I was pretty sure that nobody in Mexico besides the police in the state of San Luis Potosí was taking any interest in us.

Another hour brought us to the city of Querétaro. I gassed up there. South of Querétaro we entered the toll road to Mexico City. Although we made good time after that, it was nearly dark when we pulled up in front of the Excelsior Hotel.

When I looked across the front seat, I realized I hadn't even asked Angela where she wanted to go. "Hey, I'm sorry, Angela. Where should I let you off?"

"One street over," she said, smiling. She almost always seemed to be smiling. She gave me directions, and I drove her where she wanted to go. The building turned out to be the Mexico City YMCA.

"Listen, I'll be finished with my business tomorrow afternoon," I said. "How about having dinner with me at the hotel tomorrow night? Then I'll be able to thank you properly for all the help you've been."

"That will be nice, Devlin. Eight o'clock?"

"Fine," I said. After she picked up her case and got out, I drove back to the hotel.

I presented myself and the suitcase at the registration desk. "You're holding a reservation for Lew Devlin," I said to the clerk. I hoped I was right. I was two days late.

The clerk didn't even have to check the reservation ledger. "Ah, yes, Señor Devlin," he said smiling. "And there is a message for you." He turned and plucked a slip of paper from the key rack behind him.

The message was a crudely printed card folded in the middle which said, *I will call again at noon tomorrow.* I breathed a sigh of relief. Jim Cartwright—or somebody—had been prepared for the possibility of a delay.

I was more tired than hungry, so I went up to my room and went to bed. I slept well. In the morning I awoke at nine o'clock feeling relaxed, and I had breakfast sent up to my room. I also ordered a copy of Mexico City's English-language newspaper, *The News.*

When I finished breakfast, I settled down in an armchair with the paper. I found I couldn't concentrate on it. I wasn't as relaxed as I'd thought. Evidently I wouldn't be relaxed until I turned the suitcase over to the five-foot-six Mexican who would tell me that he's "come for the paper."

The phone call came at one minute past noon. I picked up the telephone. "Yes?" I said.

"Devlin?"

"That's right."

"Finally. An hour from now okay?"

"I'll be here."

The phone clicked in my ear.

The knock came at exactly one o'clock. I unlocked the door and a man stepped inside quickly. I closed the door behind him and turned around. He was about five feet ten and he wasn't Mexican. Of course, my being late could account for the change. I waited for him to ask me if I had brought the paper.

He didn't ask. And suddenly I knew he wasn't the right man.

He realized that I knew and smoothly pulled a gun from his coat pocket. He smiled a nasty smile. "There was a password, right?" I didn't say anything. "The little Mexican gave up the room number here, but he didn't give up the password. He kept saying there wasn't one. Which is bad luck for you." The gun was leveled directly at me. "Where's the money?"

I didn't say anything. His face darkened, and he pushed the weapon a foot closer in my direction. "Where's—"

There was a knock at the door, and a woman's voice said timidly, "Señor?"

"Who's that?" he demanded.

"I don't know," I said. "It could be the maid."

He waved the gun. "Over against the wall." I moved where he was pointing. He moved, too, in line with the door so that he was half-shielded by it as it opened slowly. He was half-turned in my direction to keep an eye on me. But he was also looking out into the hallway. The gun was behind his back.

The door opened, and he stared at who-ever was there. I couldn't see who it was. Then he gave a little bow. "Some other time, sis," he said. "This is a business meeting. But why don't you come back later and—"

He never got to finish it. A pistonlike leg came through the partly opened door and hit him squarely in the throat. I recognized the shoe. The man flew backward across the room, banging the back of his head against the opposite wall. He came off the wall grabbing for the gun that had popped out of his hand.

By that time I was right in front of him. I ignored the gun and punched the guy twice, an inch above his belt buckle. He fluttered down to the floor as if his bones had turned to water. When I turned, Angela was picking up the gun. She put it in her handbag, and I heard it clunk against something that could only have been another gun. She turned then to close and lock the door. As she did, I saw the door across the hallway standing open.

"You were stashed across the hallway," I said numbly.

Angela ignored the statement. She was glaring at the man on the floor. "Make him tell you what he did with Bedoya," she ordered me.

"Bedoya?"

"The agent who was supposed to make the meet with you."

Suddenly I saw everything. Or almost everything. "You're an agent, too, aren't you? Jim Cartwright put a tail on me. You're—"

"Make him talk, will you?" she said impatiently.

It took dumping a couple of glasses of water on him to get him focused again. I knelt down beside him. His eyes were glazed, but I was sure he could hear me. "Listen closely, pal. You didn't get the room number from Bedoya by asking him politely. I'll ask you one time. Where is Bedoya?"

I could see his throat working, but nothing came out. It would be our luck if he wanted to spill his rotten little heart out and couldn't speak. I went through his pockets. He had no wallet and no identification of any kind.

The guy was staring at Angela as if he were hypnotized. Finally his throat worked again. "Shirt pocket," he whispered.

I dug a piece of notepaper out of his shirt pocket. Written on it was what looked like an address. I handed it to Angela. She nodded. "I know where this is. It's in the warehouse district." She started ripping sheets from the bed. "Help me wrap him up."

I removed his coat first, and then we made a mummy out of him. "We'll be back," Angela threatened him, "if Bedoya isn't at this address." The guy just rolled his eyes.

I put on the coat. It was too short and too tight across the shoulders. "Somebody at that address is used to seeing this coat," I explained to Angela. "It might gain us a step or two. What about the suitcase?" I pointed to where it was, under the bed.

She frowned. "We take it with us," she decided.

"Into the lions' den?"

"If they're as toothless as this one, I don't see any problem," she informed me.

We took the car we'd been using to the warehouse. It was a cement two-story building. The ground-floor door was unlocked. I eased it open cautiously. The place looked deserted, but you couldn't tell for sure. There was a flight of iron stairs to our right. I started up the stairs. Angela was behind me. She had a gun in her hand.

Halfway up I could see there was a glass peephole in the door at the top. I stopped a step below it, and then I knocked. When I saw light behind the peephole, I turned my head away. The guy inside couldn't see much of my face, but he could see the coat. He opened the door.

I went through it in a scrambling slide. The man inside was lanky. I had him in a bear hug before he knew the score. Angela was right behind me, sweeping the small room with her gun. There was no one else there except a bundle in a corner which was a bound and gagged man.

I picked up my lanky opponent and body-slammed him. His lights went out. I gave him a fast frisk and came up with no gun but with a mean-looking knife. I tossed it to Angela, who hurried across the room and cut free the tied-up man. He sat up slowly. His face and head were a little scuffed up, but he was smiling weakly.

I pulled the suitcase into the room from where Angela had left it standing inside the door. Then Angela and I spent 15 minutes rubbing the circulation back into Bedoya's semiparalyzed legs. We helped him downstairs, and we all got into the car. With the suitcase.

Bedoya gave us the address. We stopped in front of a place that didn't look much different from the one we'd just left. The sign said, FREIGHT FORWARDING. Inside, Bedoya put the suitcase into an enormous safe. Then he sat down and wrote me a receipt.

"It will come up a touch short," I said. "There was an accident—"

"My report will cover that," Angela interrupted me.

"Blame it on me," I told her.

She shook her head. "Circumstances beyond anyone's control." She smiled and said, "Cartwright's a hard sell, but he might buy that."

There didn't seem to be anything else to say, so we took Bedoya to a doctor.

Angela and I had dinner at the Excelsior that evening. "You sandbagged me in the first inning of the ball game," I said.

"Please sit down if you like." I imitated the way she had said that to me in the coffee shop at the mining company airstrip.

She laughed. "How could I pass up such a gorgeous opportunity? Besides, all's well that ends well."

"The middle part was no waltz."

"Your job was to get the suitcase to the Excelsior. My job was to see that the transfer was made to the right person. We both did our jobs."

"And what was the whole thing about?"

"Cartwright thought there was a leak in the Washington office. The transfer was bait. It looks as though he was right, doesn't it?"

"*We* were bait, you mean."

"We did our jobs," she said. "And you should remember one other thing."

"What's that?"

"Neither of us could have done it without the other."

I picked up my glass. "I'll drink to that."

We clinked glasses across the table.